First published in Great Britain by
HarperCollins Publishers Ltd in 1996

1 3 5 7 9 10 8 6 4 2

© Nick Butterworth 1996

A CIP record for this title is
available from the British Library.
The author asserts the moral right to
be identified as the author of the work.

ISBN: 0 00 198131 5

Printed and bound in Italy

THE TREASURE HUNT

NICK BUTTERWORTH

Collins

An Imprint of HarperCollinsPublishers

"Good morning!" said Percy the park keeper as he stepped out of his hut. In his hand, Percy was holding some posters which he had just made. He pinned one of them to his door.

"What does it say?" asked one of Percy's rabbit friends.

"Oh, I'm sorry," said Percy, and he read out loud. . .

I am organising a
Treasure Hunt
All those who would like to come meet at the bandstand after breakfast, tomorrow morning.
signed Percy (Me).

"I want to come," said the badger.
"So do I," said the fox. "What is it?"

"It's a game," said Percy. "One person goes off and leaves a trail of clues for the others to follow. The clues are messages, and one clue leads to the next one until you find the treasure at the end."

"I can read a bit," said the fox. He and the other animals stared at another of Percy's posters. Percy smiled as he noticed they were holding it upside down.

"I'll do drawings instead of messages," he said.

Next morning, when the animals met together, there was no sign of Percy. They thought that Percy must have forgotten, until one of the squirrels noticed something.

"Look! There's a piece of paper with a picture on it. It could be a clue."

The squirrel was right. On the paper, Percy had drawn a picture of a see-saw.

"That must be where we have to go first," said the badger.

They hurried over to the playground.
Sure enough, another piece of paper
had been pinned to the see-saw.

"I'll get it," said one of the mice and he
scampered up the see-saw.

This time Percy had drawn
a picture of a statue.
"I know where that is,"
said a rabbit. "Follow me!"
And off they went again.

By now, Percy had put nearly all his pieces of paper in place. He whistled as he walked along a favourite path at the edge of the park.

"Only two left," said Percy as he tucked one of his clues into a crack in a signpost.

He stopped for a moment and gazed over the fields which lay beyond the park.

Percy reached into his pocket and was pleased to find some chocolate. It was chocolate money, wrapped in gold paper.

"A good job I brought a snack," said Percy, "I'm feeling quite peckish."
Slowly he ate every piece of the chocolate.

Then Percy realised
what he had done.
He had eaten
the treasure.

The animals were having great fun. Percy's trail of clues lead them all over the park.

The see-saw. The statue. The tool shed. The bridge. In every place they found a picture showing them where to go next.

ut now, as they searched for a clue around a signpost at the edge of the park, it didn't seem quite so easy.

"Bother," said the badger. "I can't see a clue anywhere."

The fox kept looking at the letters on the signpost. He was sure they were trying to tell him something.

"I wonder. . ." he muttered to himself.

Suddenly the fox announced, "this signpost is the next clue. We have to follow it."

"But it leads out of the park," said the hedgehog.

It was too late. The fox had already set off. The others looked at each other, then they followed after him.

The fox lead them across a field. In the middle, there stood a tall tree which had been struck by lightning.

Further on, there was a cattle shelter. Something was moving behind it.

"It looks like Percy," said the fox. "That must be where he's putting the treasure."

The animals rushed towards the cattle shelter.

It wasn't Percy. But there was something there, and the something said. . .

"Mooo!"

"You won't find any clues up there," chuckled Percy. "Why don't you come down and meet Lucy?"

The animals scrambled up the tree as fast as they could. They didn't like this game at all.

"What do we do now?" wailed the hedgehog.

He was answered by someone who had been watching it all.

Lucy the calf was very friendly. When the animals had calmed down and been properly introduced, she gave them a ride across the field to the park fence.

Everyone chattered happily as they bumped along.

"We didn't find the treasure," said the fox, "but we found a friend."

Percy coughed and wiped the corner of his mouth with his handkerchief.

"And don't you think friends are better than treasure?" he said.

It was a young calf.
"Mmmoo!" said the calf loudly again.
The animals squealed and ran in fright
towards the tree in the middle of the field.

The calf chased after them.
She wanted to play.

"Well," said the hedgehog, "I think they're about the same."

Percy smiled.

"I think you're right," he said.

Percy doesn't know that he dropped three pieces
of the treasure on his way around the park.
Can you find them?